# COUNTRY MUSIC
# MOON
## Awards

CMMA

PUBLISHED BY
OXVISION
BOOKS

ILLUSTRATED BY **TIM LADWIG** & WRITTEN BY **BRIAN OXLEY**

ISBN 978 1 938068 36 2

Library of Congress Control Number: 2019941500

Published by Oxvision Books
4001 Tamiami Trail North, Suite 250, Naples, FL 34103

Find us at: oxvisionmedia.com

# COUNTRY MUSIC

# MOON

*Awards*

Ivy had a secret. Yes, many more people would hear her music than the travelers from earth to moon for the awards performances. But she would be the only earth person to know.

COUNTRY MUSIC

# MOON

*Awards*

CMMA

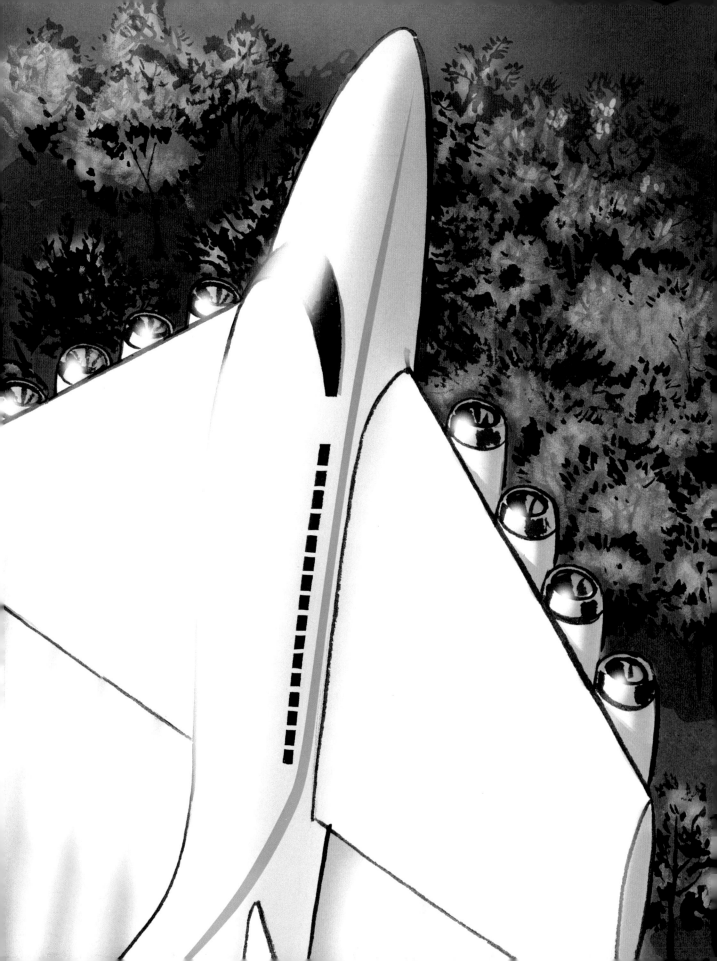

As the moon transport took off from Johnny Cash's farm in Tennessee, Ivy held a container of water from the spring in the woods. It was her present for Teardrops, the little Moon Being she met on her last visit.

After sailing past satellites, asteroids, and meteors, they landed on moon's surface. As the gray dust settled, Ivy spotted a small rock sliding toward the ship. Ivy knew this was no rock. It was Teardrops!

Ivy slipped away while everyone else was taking their baggage to the Music Awards Village. She followed her friend behind a large boulder.

Teardrops pushed a hidden button, and a large rock slid to the side. Below was a world no human had ever seen! Teardrops held Ivy's hand, and together they jumped.

Down they descended—past floating gardens and waterfalls and beautiful birds that glided by on graceful, outspread wings. Ivy took off her helmet and breathed in the sweet-scented air.

True to her name, Teardrops began to cry. Tears of joy. Like the first time they met, Ivy could hear in her mind what Teardrops was saying, "I am so happy to see you!" Moon tears and earth tears flowed together.

All the beauty overwhelmed Ivy. Then her
dream came true. She danced mid-air.
Only instead of ballet, a new dance—the
"floating line dance."

She even taught Teardrops and the birds,
and they joined in!

Suddenly, Ivy heard a tremendous sound
as the Moon Beings clapped their stone
suits with stone drumsticks in applause.

"That was wonderful," Teardrops said. "Now it's your turn for something new." Floating to a nearby tree, Teardrops picked a piece of fruit. It gave off a golden glow and was sweeter and more delicious than anything Ivy had tasted.

Then Ivy saw a purple tree with amazing-looking fruit. Teardrops explained that the Moon Beings had been forbidden to eat from it. "If even one person would eat the fruit of this tree, the moon would become like the earth with wars, hate, pollution, and lies."

As they floated on, Ivy was amazed at how all the moon animals lived together peacefully. The large, fierce-looking ones lay next to the small, cuddly ones, and they all ate moon grass together.

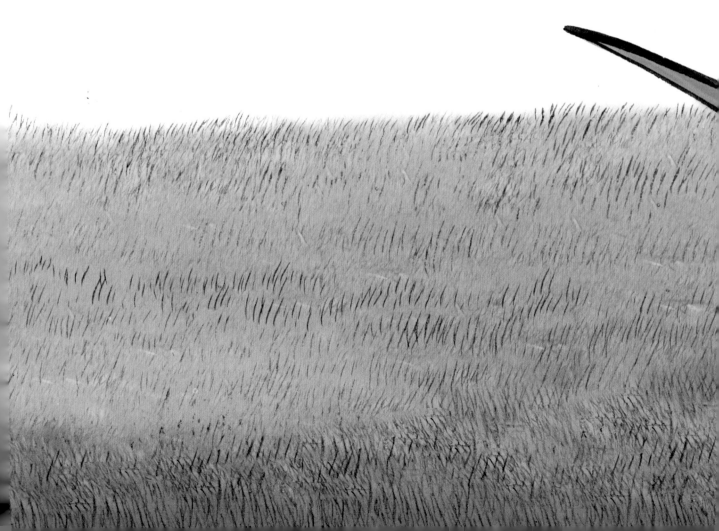

Then Teardrops showed Ivy a special
window the Moon Beings used to observe
important events of mankind. Sometimes
they saw the sad things like sickness,
hunger, war, and pollution.

They also watched and listened
to earth musicians, especially
Johnny Cash, their favorite.

Teardrops motioned to a floating
stage under the window. A beautiful black
guitar on a stand was set in the center.

"We made this guitar just like the one
Johnny Cash played. We hoped that
someday, someone from earth would
come sing one of his songs."

Then Ivy saw that all around the stage people had gathered in floating chairs.

"They've come to hear you sing, Ivy," said Teardrops. "Would you honor us by performing one of Johnny's songs?"

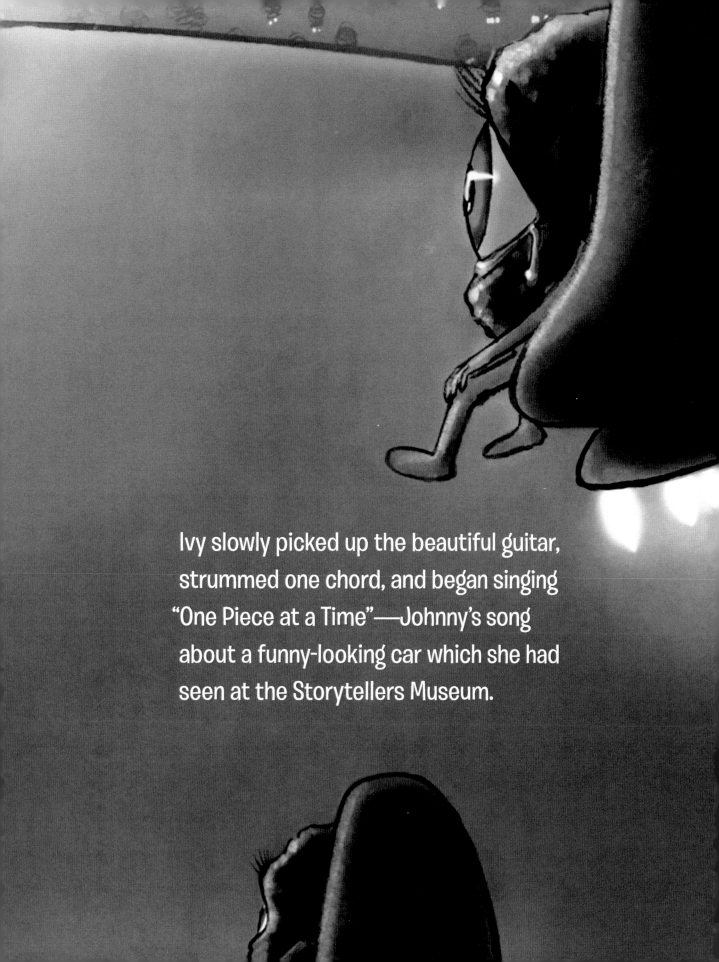

Ivy slowly picked up the beautiful guitar, strummed one chord, and began singing "One Piece at a Time"—Johnny's song about a funny-looking car which she had seen at the Storytellers Museum.

The Moon Beings understood Ivy's every
word and cried with excitement upon
hearing the music they loved being sung
by an Earthling live for the first time.

Of course, the band and contestants who were on the surface were completely unaware of the magical world just below.

Then Ivy sang "Will the Circle Be Unbroken?" The Moon Beings welcomed its message of hope and gave her a standing ovation.

Ivy knew her band would be looking for her, so Teardrops led her back to the surface.

That night Ivy won the Country Music Moon Award for Best Entertainer as audiences above and below the moon's surface looked on and applauded.

As Ivy looked out the window and watched the moon get smaller and smaller, she was both happy and sad. Sad because she would miss her new friends. Happy because she knew one day she would return and would sing for Teardrops and the Moon Beings again.

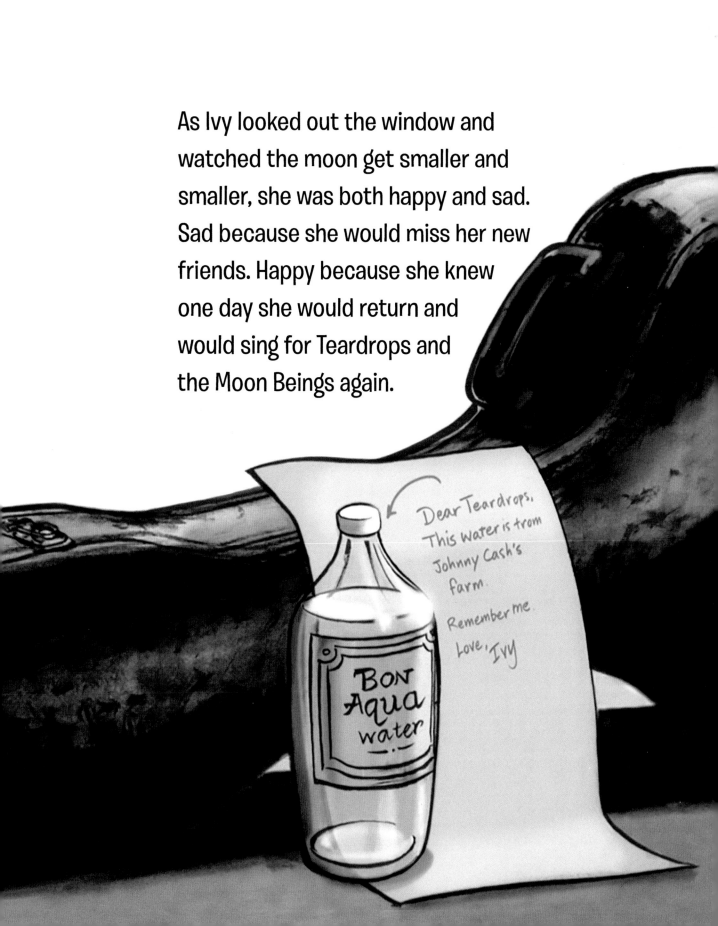

The End.

# Follow
# GRANDPA
## on his many adventures...

*Find these books and others at oxvisionmedia.com or your favorite online retailer.*

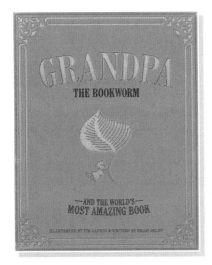

**GRANDPA THE BOOKWORM AND THE WORLD'S MOST AMAZING BOOK**

**GRANDPA, HOW BIG IS YOUR LOVE?**

**GRANDPA'S DIET**

**GRANDPA'S TIMEOUT**

**GRANDPA SAVES THE DAY**

**GRANDPA'S OVERALLS**

# More Oxvision Books
## for Young Readers

**GRANDPA, THE MUSIC EXECUTIVE**

**ON-TIME GRANDPA**

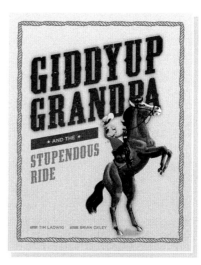

**GIDDYUP GRANDPA AND
THE STUPENDOUS RIDE**

**GRANDPA'S MOON GAMES**

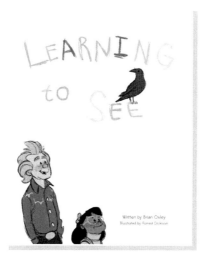

**LEARNING TO SEE**

**W.S. "FLUKE" HOLLAND:
THE FATHER OF THE DRUMS**

OXVISION
BOOKS

Made in the USA
Middletown, DE
12 August 2019